This Gift of Reading
is Donated By

*People Who Read Achieve*℠

Rupert the Reader
and your neighborhood
7-Eleven store.

# THE WATERTOWER

GARY CREW

STEVEN WOOLMAN

# THE WATERTOWER

Written by
GARY CREW

Illustrated by
STEVEN WOOLMAN

*for Janet*

*Nobody in Preston could remember when the watertower was built, or who had built it, but there it stood on Shooters Hill — its iron legs rusted, its egg-shaped tank warped and leaking — casting a long, dark shadow across the valley, across Preston itself.*

First American edition published 1998 by

**Crocodile Books, USA**
An imprint of Interlink
Publishing Group, Inc.
99 Seventh Avenue
Brooklyn, New York 11215

Text © Gary Crew 1994, 1998
Illustrations © Era Publications 1994, 1998

Design and illustration by Steven Woolman
Produced by Martin International Pty Ltd
Originally published in Australia by
Era Publications

**Library of Congress
Cataloging-in-Publication Data**

Crew, Gary, 1947-
    The watertower / written by Gary
Crew ; illustrated by Steven Woolman. —
1st American ed.
        p.  cm.
    Summary: On a scorching hot
summer day in Preston, Australia, Spike
and Bubba go for a swim in the old water
tower which casts a long dark shadow
across everything in the area.
    ISBN 1-56656-233-3 (hardcover)
    [1. Water towers—Fiction.  2.
Friendship—Fiction.  3. Australia Fiction.]
I. Woolman, Steven, 1969-  ill.  II. Title.

PZ7.C867Wat  1998
[E]—dc21                         97-23095
                                      CIP
                                       AC

Printed in Hong Kong

Crocodile
Books, USA

One summer afternoon, Spike Trotter met
Bubba D'Angelo by the service station and
together they went up to the tower for a swim.

Spike led the way, as usual.
"My mother says it's dangerous up there,"
he said, "but it's worth it, hey?"

Bubba puffed on behind. His mother couldn't
have cared less where he went.

At the summit, Spike stopped
to look down on the sweltering
town. "Suckers," he grinned,
and headed for the tower.

Last summer, a security fence
had kept trespassers out,
but now the metal posts were
twisted and flattened and barbed
wire lay coiled on the ground.

"You reckon vandals done that?" Bubba asked, recovering his breath.

But Spike was already on the top. "Hurry up," he yelled, throwing open the access hatch. "It's scorching up here."

He pulled his shirt over his head, dropped his shorts and clambered down into the tank.

t was dark inside. "The dark's got a sort
of a color," Bubba said, squatting on the
bottom rung of the ladder. "It's sort of
green. Like moss. Like slimy, dead moss."

Spike didn't answer. Except for the
ghostly wailing he kept up for the fun of
hearing the echo, he might not have been
there at all.

"Spike?" Bubba called. "Spikey?" Still no
answer; so Bubba whistled for a while,
then splashed a bit — but only up to his
knees. He didn't particularly like the water.
He wasn't keen on slipping down, naked,
into its murky dark. And from time to time
he glanced up at the shaft of sunlight
angling in from the open hatch, imagining

At last, Bubba called, "Spikey, I'm going up now. I'm going to get dressed."

He guessed that Spike was somewhere beneath him, in the water that eddied and swirled.

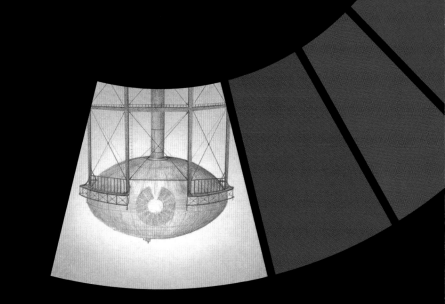

Bubba stepped out on to the top of the tank. The wind was hot; the glare terrible. Blinking and squinting, he looked about for his towel. It had blown to the far side of the tank and hung there, caught on the head of a valve. "Maybe I should have stayed down," he muttered to himself, tiptoeing across the burning metal. With the towel wrapped around him, he looked for his clothes. Spike's were there, wedged beneath the hatch, and he saw his shirt flapping at the top of the ladder. But where were his shorts?

He turned around and around. Nothing. He dropped on his hands and knees and crept to the side of the tank, yelping with each movement as the burning surface seared. He peered over the side. Nothing.

He made his way back to the hatch, calling, "Hey, are my pants down there?"

"What?" came the response.

He repeated the question, then waited, standing on his crumpled shirt, keeping his towel tight around him. Spike's dripping head suddenly appeared. "Nope," he spluttered. "Nothing's down there but water," and he pulled himself free of the dark.

Bubba looked about him again. "Then they've blown away. That's what happened, I bet."

Spike laughed. "Doesn't matter," he said, shaking himself and reaching for his clothes. "You've got your towel. Go home in that."

Bubba shook his head. "No way. If my mother finds out that I lost my pants, I'm dead."

They looked at each other. They knew that this was true. Mama D'Angelo could land a wallop like nobody else in town.

"I'll go back," Spike volunteered. "I'll run the whole way. I'll sneak in through your bedroom window and get another pair. Top drawer of your dresser. Right?"

Bubba nodded. "I'll wait here. I'll get back down, out of the sun. Will you . . . Will you be long?"

Spike was already on the ladder. "I didn't win the cross-country for nothing, did I? I'll run . . ."

His last words were lost in the wind.

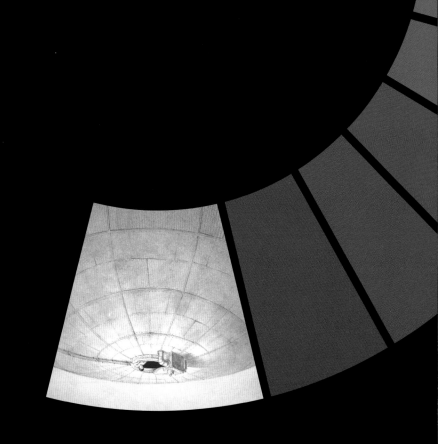

Bubba climbed into the tank. "I'll be all right," he muttered. "I'll be all right." But when he looked, the bottom rung was a long way from the light. And the water seemed darker. So he stopped halfway, and waited.

All about him the tower creaked and groaned. *That's the heat,* he reasoned. *The heat expanding the metal.*

There was a smell. *That's the algae. All rotten and festering.*

The water eddied and swirled. *That's the wind shifting the tower. It's old and rickety.*

But he was frightened, very frightened and, rung by rung — so as not to shake the ladder, not to disturb anything — he crept upwards, towards the sun.

When Bubba reached the top, he lifted himself out and squatted a moment, catching his breath, calming his heart. "I'll get off this stupid thing," he said. "I'll go and wait in the bushes."

So he did. He tightened the towel around his stomach, climbed down the outside ladder and hopped across the burning earth to the patchy shade of a gray-leafed bush.

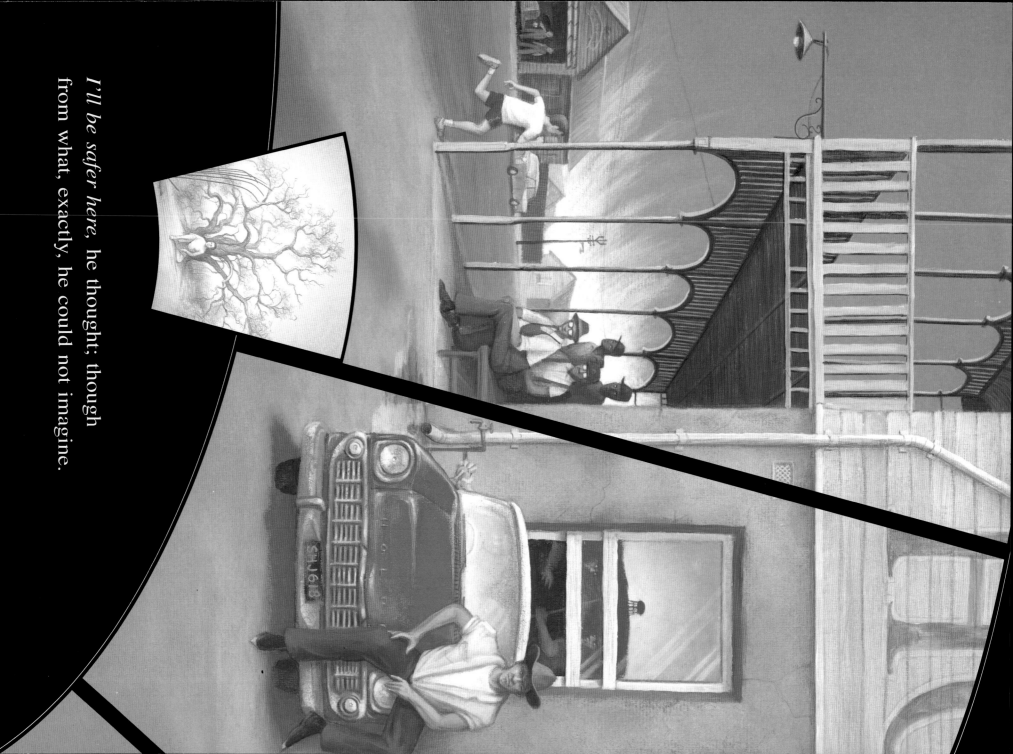

*I'll be safer here, he thought; though from what, exactly, he could not imagine.*

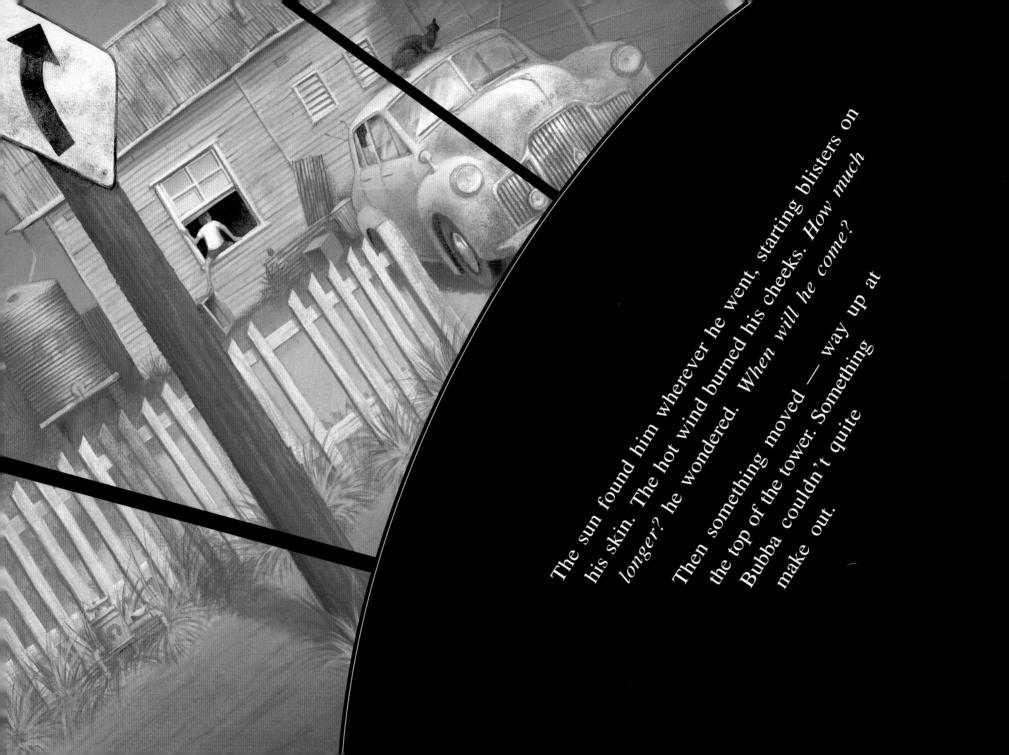

The sun found him wherever he went, starting blisters on his skin. The hot wind burned his cheeks. *How much longer?* he wondered. *When will he come?*

Then something moved — way up at the top of the tower. Something Bubba couldn't quite make out.

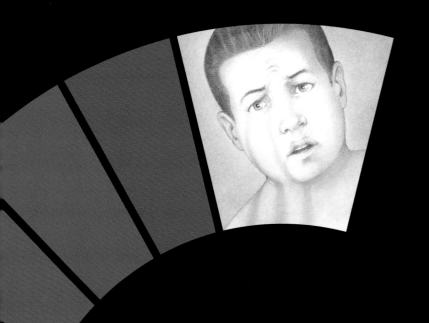

"Spike?" Bubba called. "Is that you?"

No answer.

"Spike?" he whispered, getting up.
"Spikey . . ."

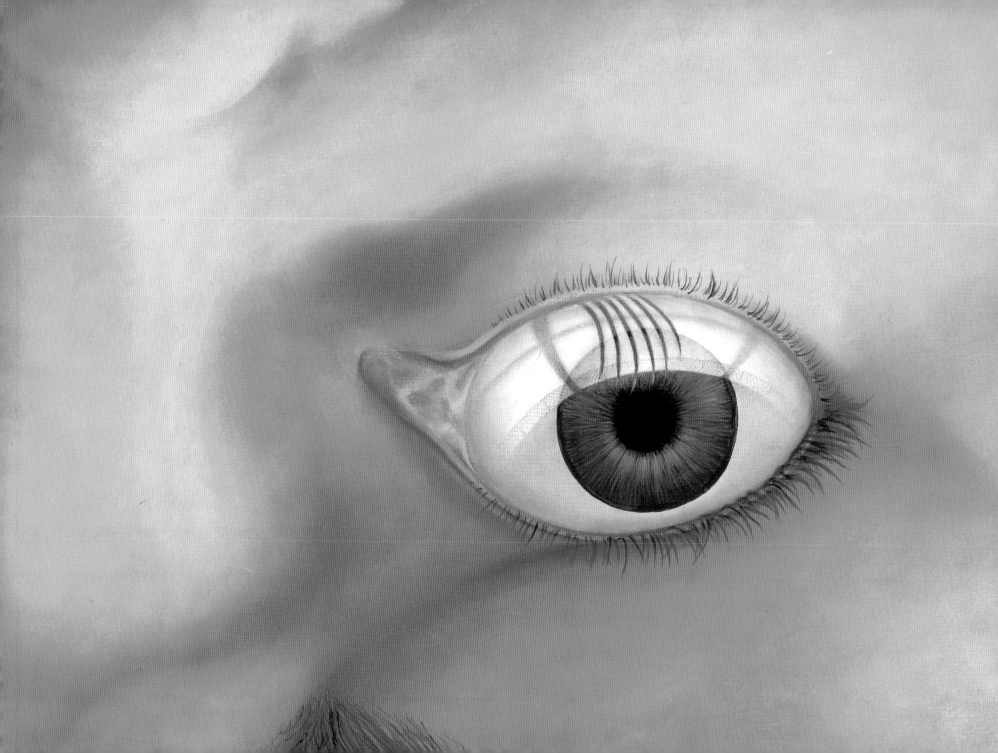

When Spike returned, calling and waving the shorts,
Bubba stuck his head straight out of the tank.
"Oh boy," he said, dressing himself, "if I stayed
down there a minute longer, I reckon I would have
dissolved. The water was great. I had the best swim.
I taught myself to lie on the bottom. I could do it
to the count of a hundred and twenty. No lie. Two
minutes. Boy that was good."

Spike's eyes narrowed. This was not like Bubba.
Not like Bubba at all. "Go on," he said, shoving him.
"Show us your fingers then; show us the water
wrinkles. Come on . . ."

Bubba turned away. "Nah. No time now," he answered. "My mother will be worried. You know what a worrier she is. She'll be scared something happened to me, won't she?" He shut the hatch with a thud.

Deep in the tank, the water eddied and swirled.